Chip had a bug.

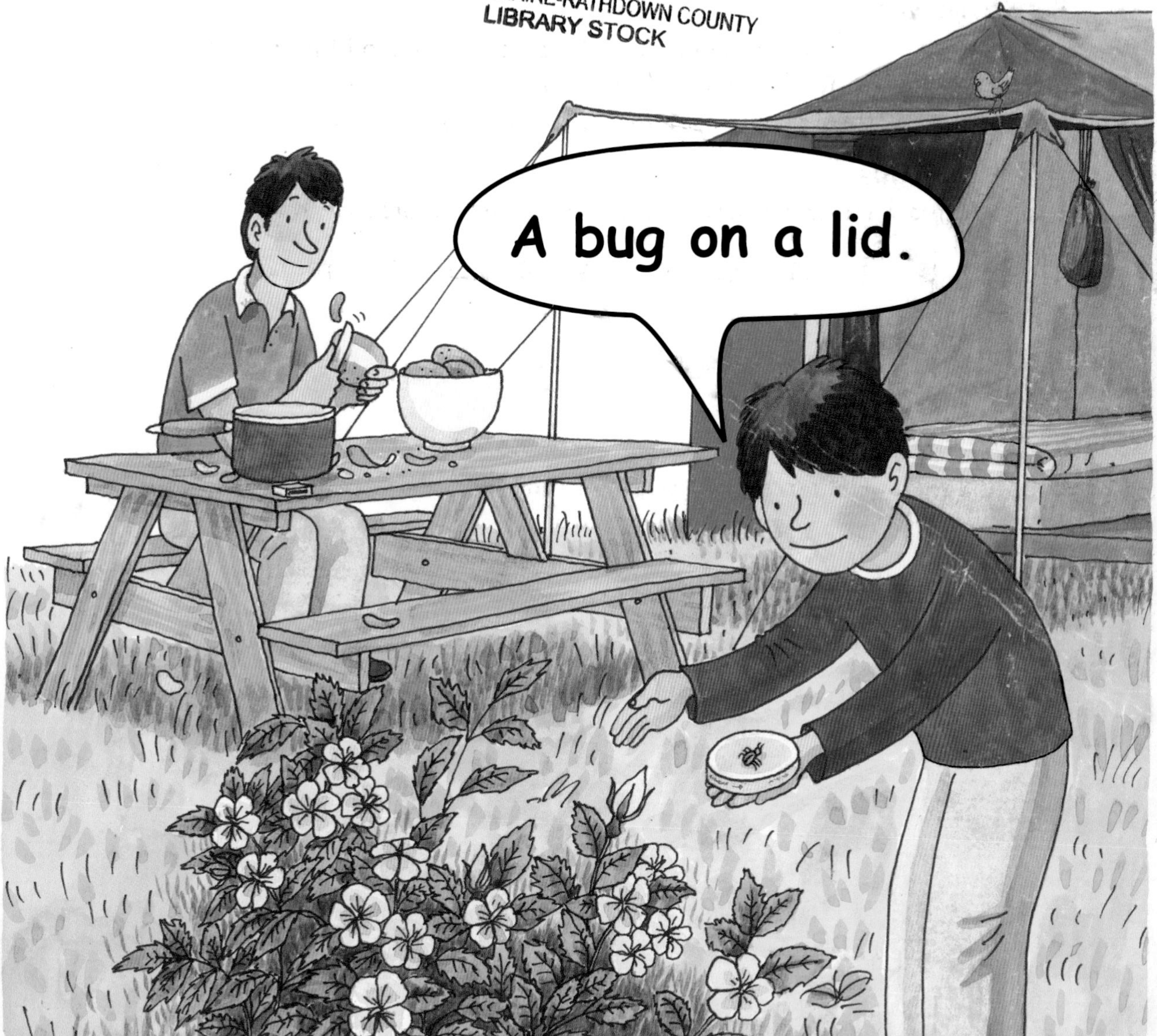

Biff had a bug.

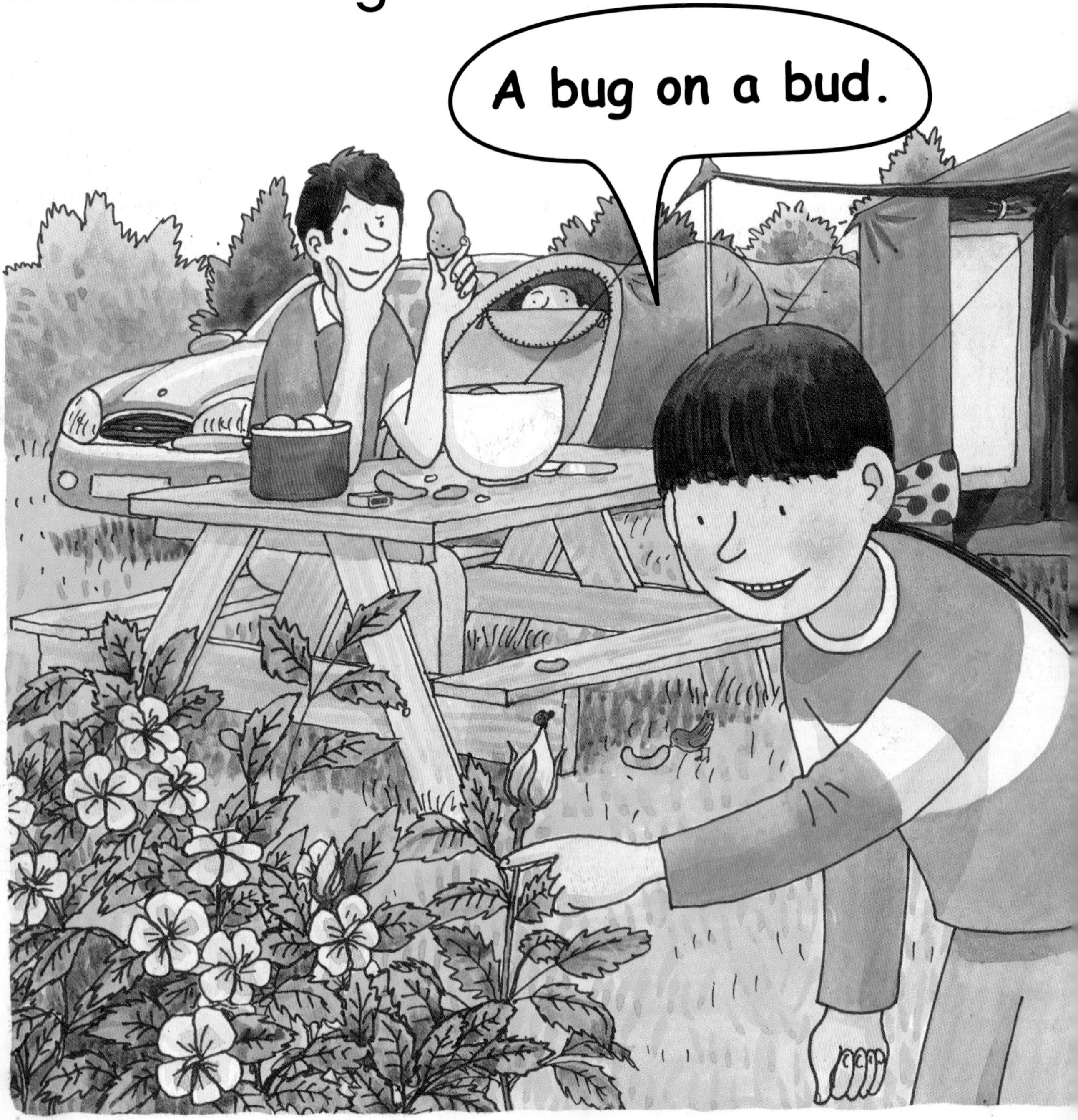

Kipper had a bug.

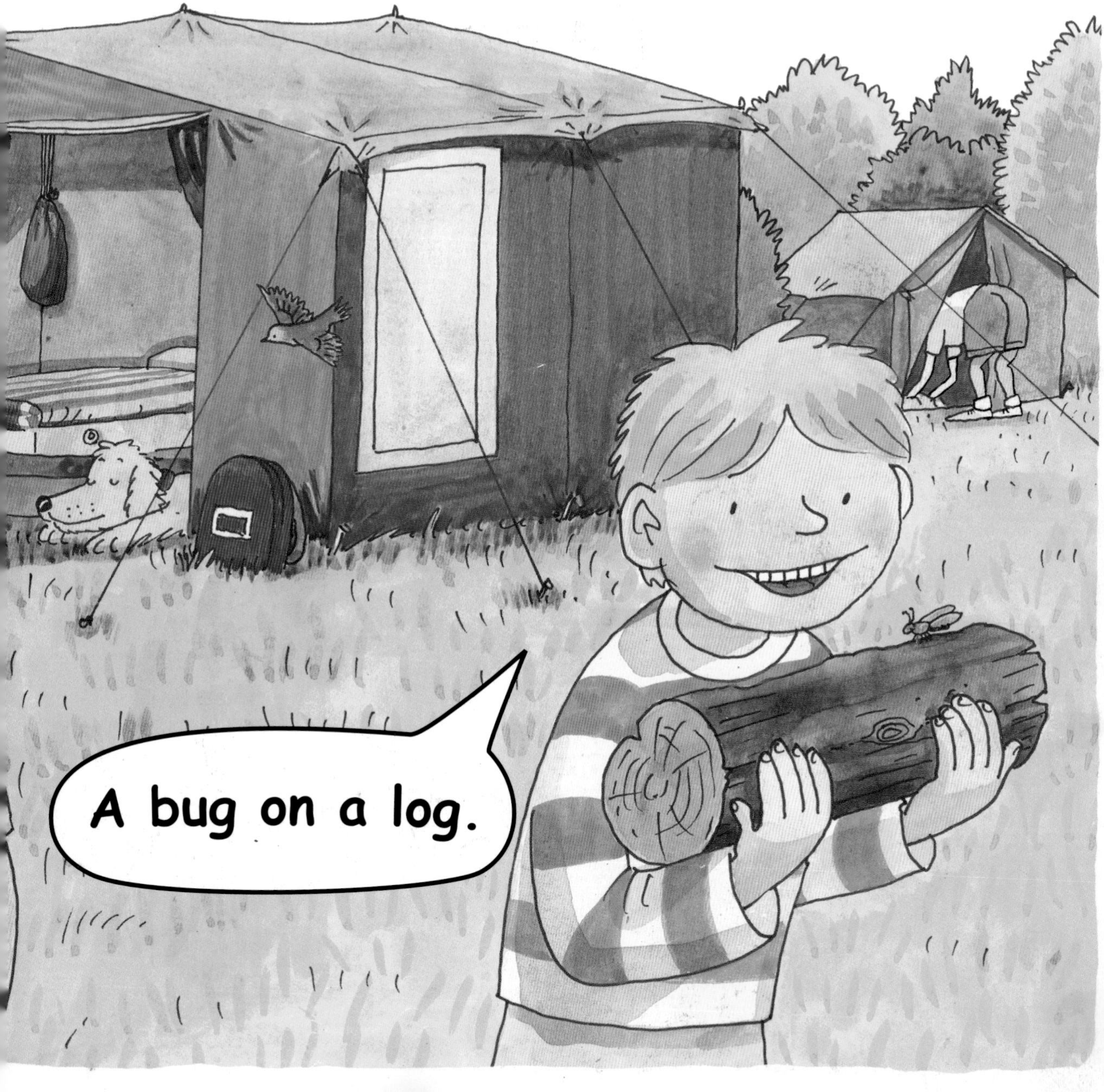

Biff had a bug in a bag.
Chip had a bug in a cup.

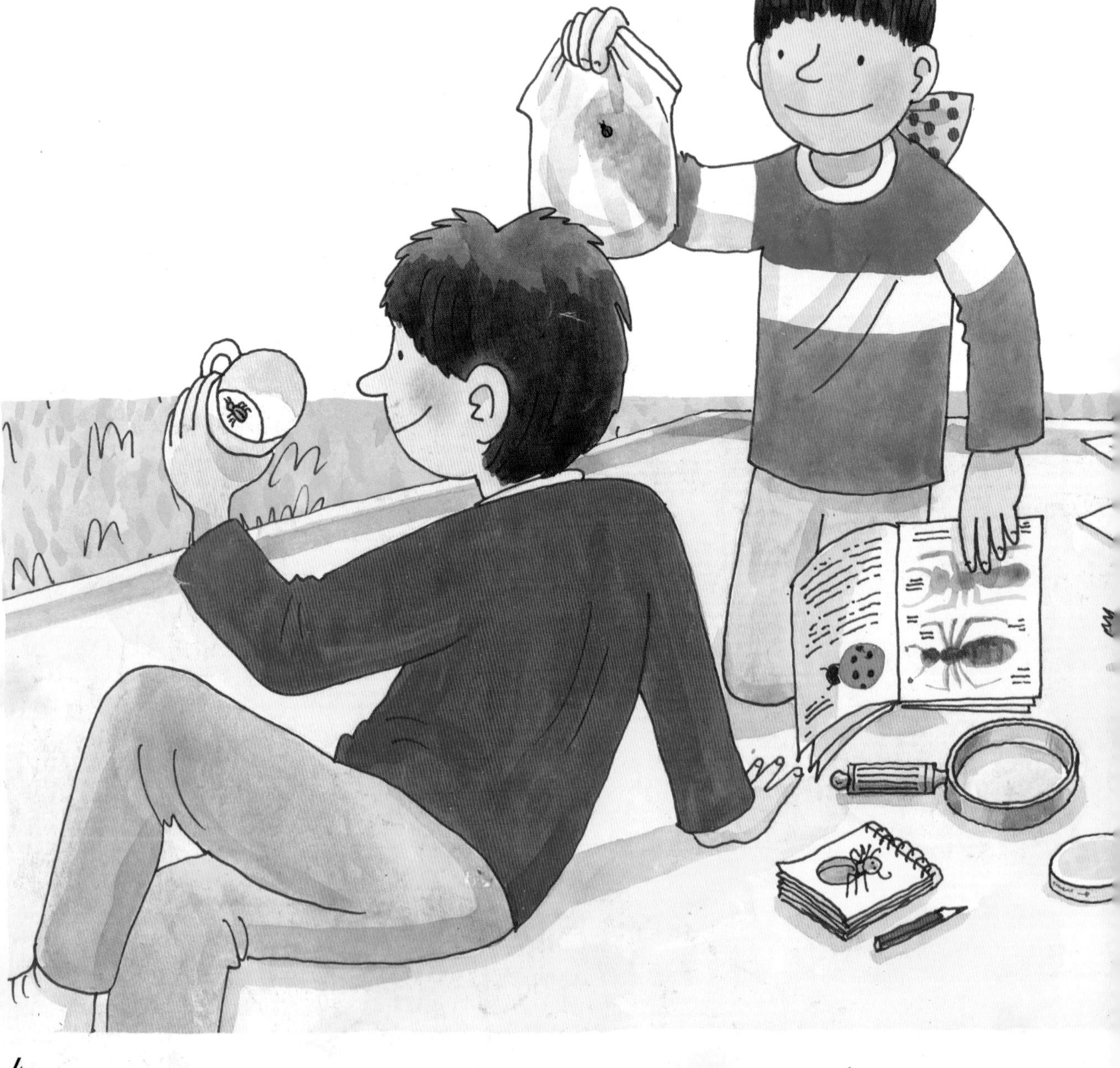

Kipper had a bug in a pot.

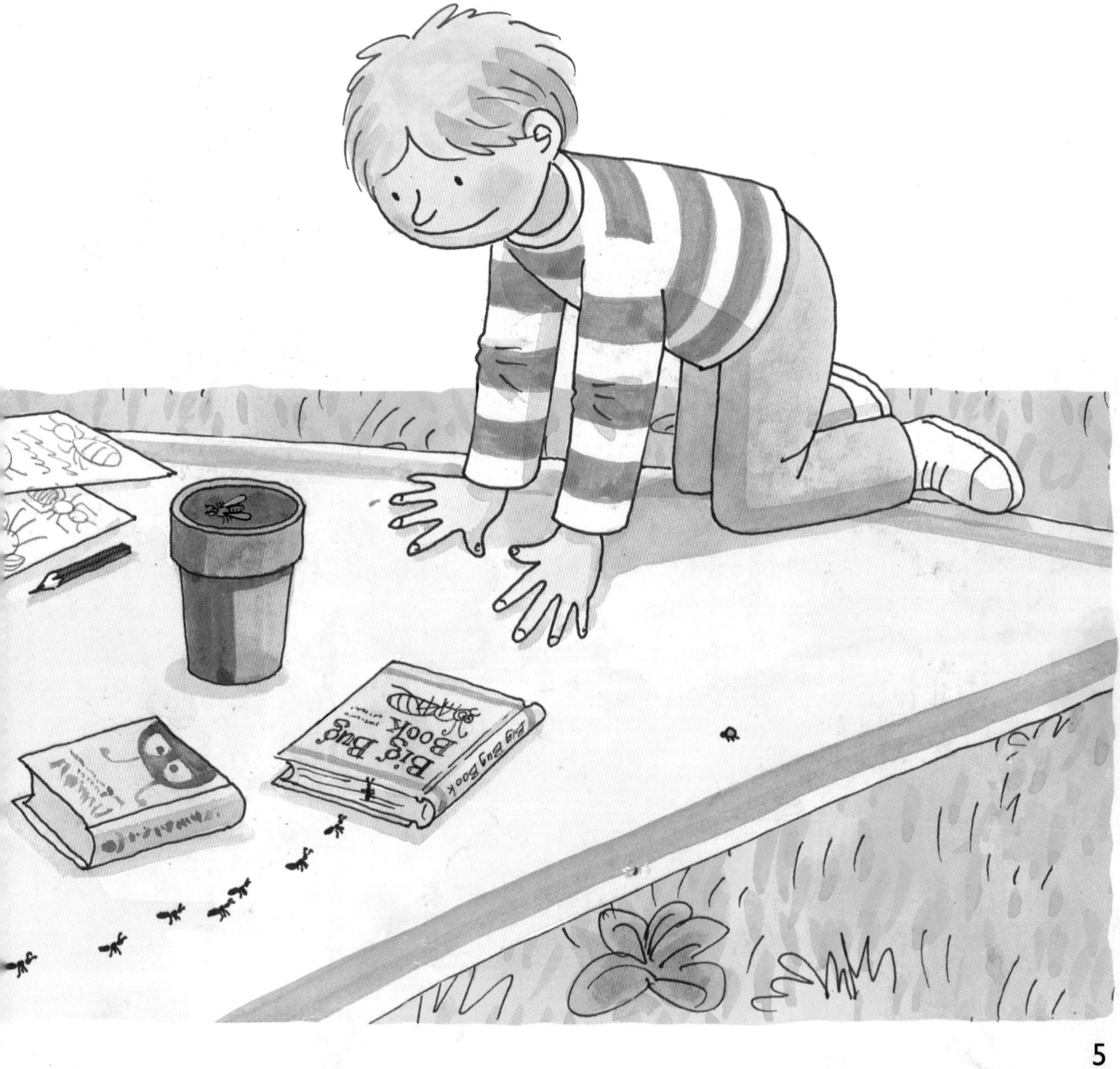

Dad had a bug . . .

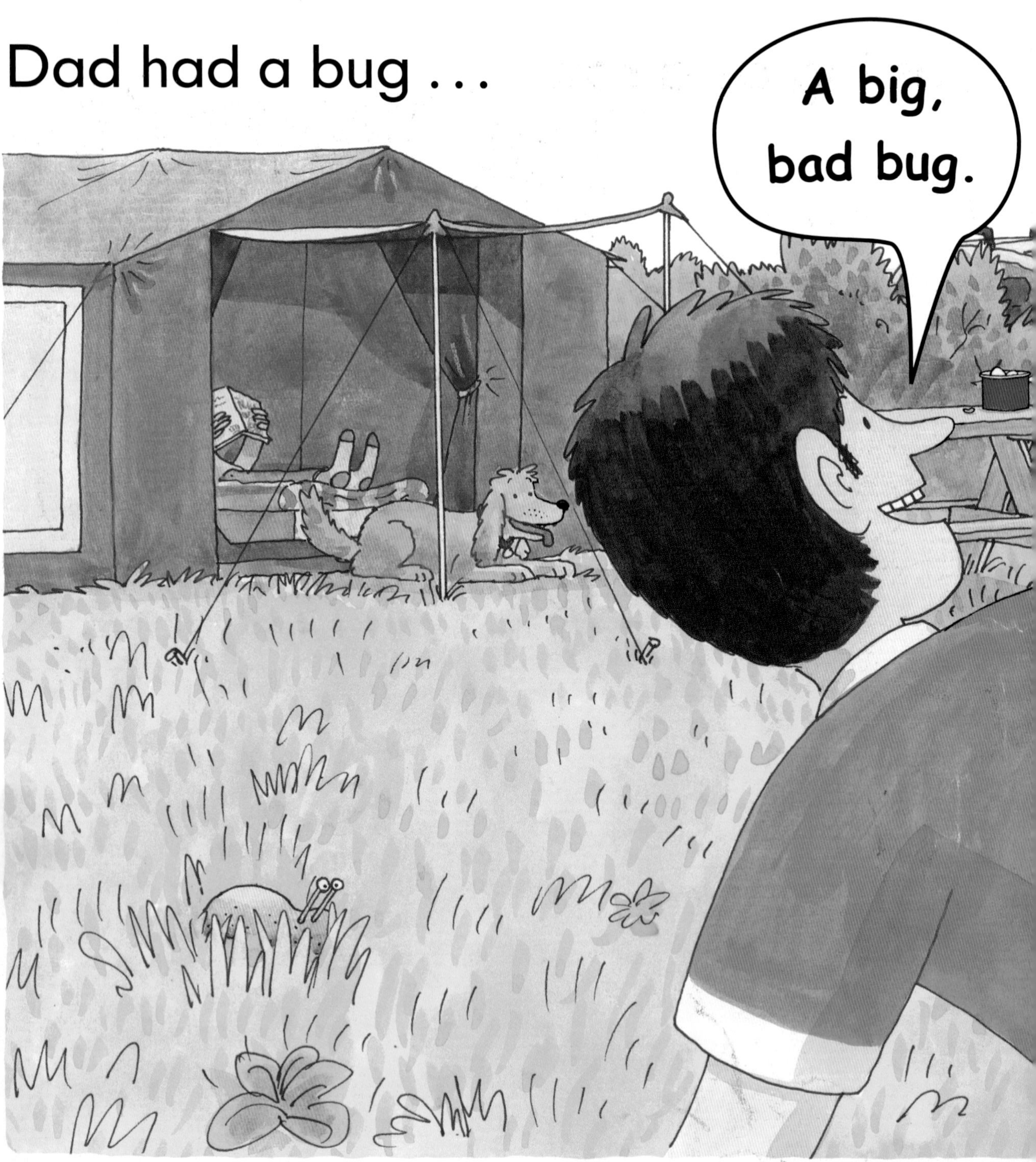

. . . as big as a rat.

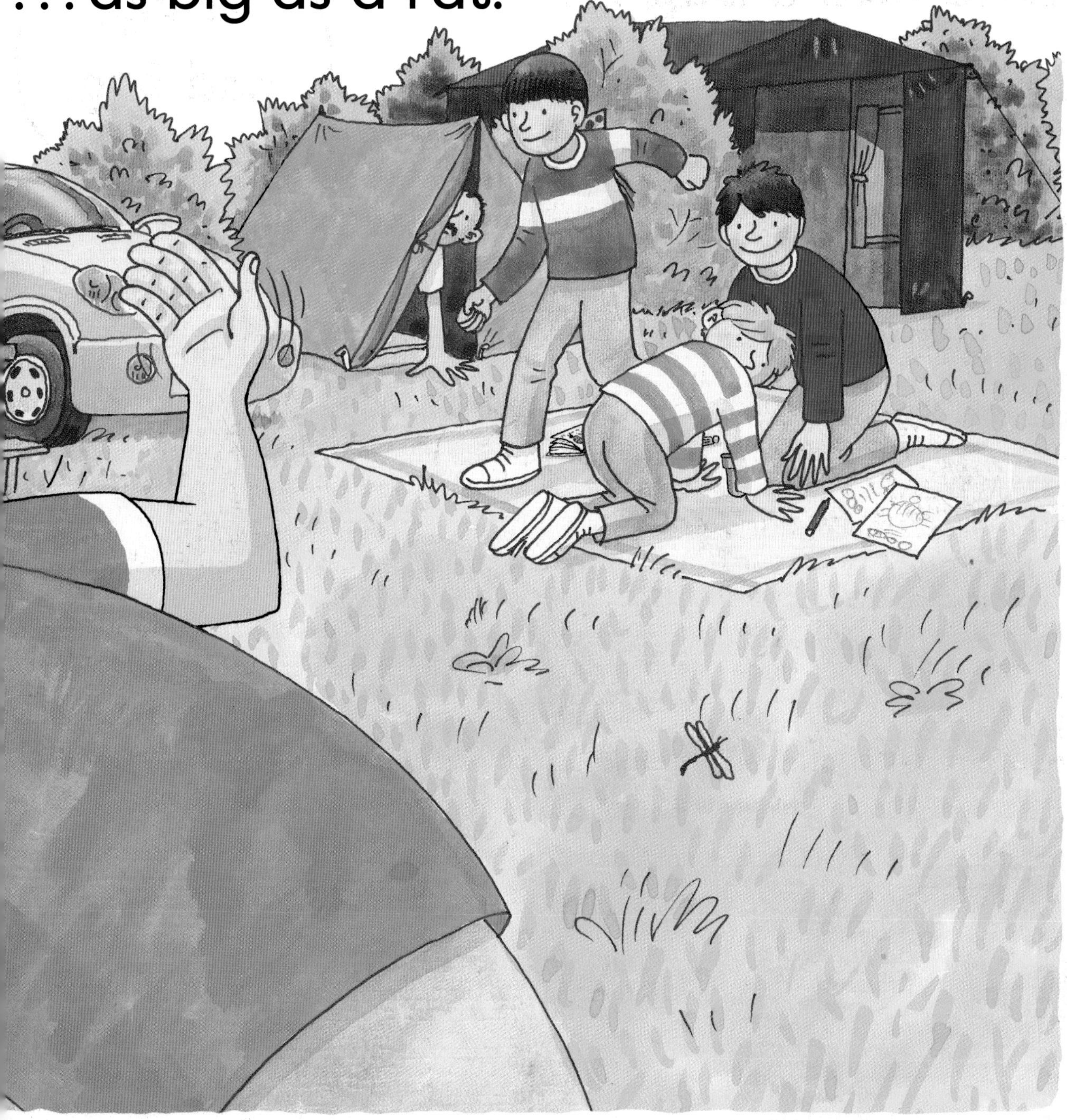

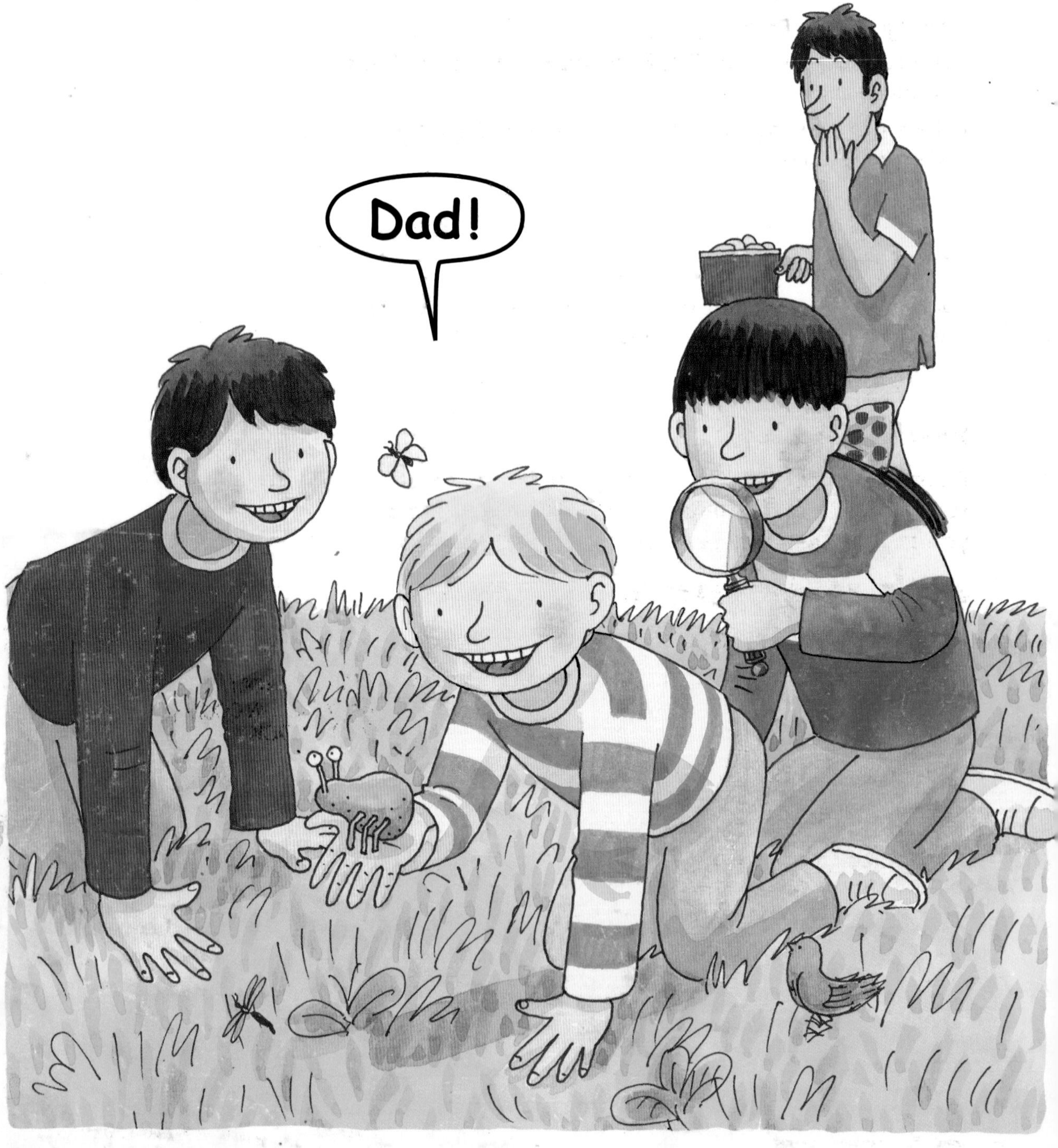
Dad!